SHARE FAIRIES

You're A Big Kid Now!

By Stefani Kauppila

Illustrated By Marcus Cutler

and painting

and sushi

BECKETT

LOVES:
space, pranks, and popsicles

DIEGO

LOVES:
science, unicorns, and playing piano

s and yo-yo's

VANESSA

LOVES:
crossword puzzles, tap dancing,
and licorice

SHIRLEY MAE

LOVES:
angels, tulips, and fairy tales

IRIS

LOVES:
biking, baking, and backpacking

ALE

LOVES:
snowboarding, rollerskating, and cookies

KAILANI

LOVES:
camping, volunta
and broccoli

GRIFFIN

OVES:
building, soccer, and fishing

KATE

LOVES:
reading, bugs, and singing

TAYE

LOVES:
highfives,

HOLLY

LOVES:
aking, reading, and gardening

NIA

LOVES:
drawing, music, and helping

MIKKO

LOVES:
hiking, snak

For our Big Kids.
We hope to inspire in you everything you inspire in us.

To the Shariest Sharers who believed in our vision and helped us
kickstart this project: Julie & Jukka Kauppila, Christine & Richard
Ryan, Melissa Bylow, Shirley Mae Brumm, Michael Radach & Linda
Morey-Radach, and Jimmy Cho. Our deepest gratitude.

For information regarding permission, write Share Fairies LLC at
contact@sharefairies.com or visit www.sharefairies.com.

Library of Congress Cataloging-in-Publication Data
Kauppila, Stefani.

Share Fairies: You're a Big Kid Now / Stefani Kauppila &
Marcus Cutler - First edition.

ISBN 978-0-578-59020-2 (hardcover)

First printing 2019

Recommended for children aged 18 months and over.

SHARE FAIRIES

You're A Big Kid Now!

By Stefani Kauppila   Illustrated By Marcus Cutler

Deep in the Land of Sharing,
magical creatures lurk.
Share Fairies frolic while
they toil, hard at work.

Singing joyous songs and
spreading shareful cheer,
To the big kids (like you)
who are big enough to hear.

NiA

GRIFFIN

Shirley Mae

"We're the Share Fairies
and we love to share.
The big kids give,
and it shows they care.

When the babies receive,
they giggle and coo.
It's time to share. We are
waiting for you!"

When it is time to choose a box, you know what to do.
You're a big kid now. Share toys you don't use.
Share those diapers and the bottles. Spit that binky out!
Get ready! Get set! Let's hear you shout!

"I'm a big kid now, and I love to share!
The babies need some help. I will show I care.
I set my items in the box. 'Goodbye,' I'll say.
Share Fairies, please come and take them away!"

With a *poof* and a flicker, Fairies appear in your room.
Digging through the box, they sigh a tiny swoon.
Sharing makes them happy. Fairies burst into song.
Even fast asleep, you will hum along:

"We're the Share Fairies and we love to share.
The big kids give, and it shows they care.
When the babies receive, they giggle and coo.
Thank you for sharing. We appreciate you!"

Scooping up the treasures are your new tiny friends.
The box is left with you. Sharing never ends!
Before they leave, a note slips under the lid.
"You are share-arific! Thank you, Big Kid!"

Soaring home to Land of Sharing. "Come on, let's hurry!"
Your donation is greeted by a fabulous fairy flurry.
Fairies clapping. Fairies cheering. Fairies singing, too.
This special sharebration is all because of YOU!

THE
SHARIEST SHARERS
Sophie Beatrix

Sorting bottles and binkies and diapers galore!
Sorting toys, sorting blankies, sorting stuffies
through each door.
Scrub and wash; organize and pack.
Add each new box to the delivery stack.

To all corners of the world, Fairies fly out to deliver.
Their Share-O-Meter needles begin to shake and quiver.
Boxes land in each crib. Share Fairies: Mission Complete!
The joy that sharing brings simply cannot be beat.

Share Fairies, they knew! The babies, they coo!
They start using the items and the toys from you!
Babies worldwide are happy and clean.
Share Fairies rejoice and again they sing:

"We're the Share Fairies and we love to share.
The big kids give, and it shows they care.
When the babies receive, they giggle and coo.
Thank you for sharing. We appreciate you!"

It's time to fill your box
all the way to the top.
Pile in your goodies until
the lid pops off!
It feels warm and fuzzy
to help others out.
Jump up and down, and
let's hear you shout:

"I'm a big kid now, and I love to share!
The babies need some help. I will show I care.
I set items in the box. 'Goodbye,' I'll say.
Share Fairies, please come and take them away!"

THIS BOX
BELONGS TO:
_____

Ideas for Parents
and Big Kids

1. Find a box, envelope,
or bag

2. Decorate and put
your name on it

3. Leave the Share
Fairies a note

4. Say "Goodbye!"
to your items

5. Learn more about the
Share Fairies at
sharefairies.com

, and painting

MAVERICK

LOVES:
flying, birds, and magic

ADELAIDE

LOVES:
boating, snorkeling, and lollipops

BECKETT

LOVES:
space, pranks, and popsicles

all, and sushi

DIEGO

LOVES:
science, unicorns, and playing piano

VANESSA

LOVES:
crossword puzzles, tap dancing, and licorice

and yo-yo's

SHIRLEY MAE

LOVES:
angels, tulips, and fairy tales

IRIS

LOVES:
biking, baking, and backpacking

ACE

LOVES:
snowboarding, rollerskating, and cookies

KAILANI

LOVES:
camping, volunte and broccoli

GRIFFIN

LOVES:
building, soccer, and fishing

KATE

LOVES:
reading, bugs, and singing

TAYE

LOVES:
highfives,

HOLLY

LOVES:
baking, reading, and gardening

NIA

LOVES:
drawing, music, and helping

MIKKO

LOVES:
hiking, snak

SHARE FAIRIES

CPSIA information can be obtained
at www.ICGtesting.com
Printed in the USA
LVHW072236060120
642736I.V00021B/254/P